Saint Jenni
Super Hero

Doctor, racing driver, ballerina, space explorer – everyone wants to do something exciting when they grow up. Including Jenni. She's aiming for the top. Jenni wants to be – a saint!

She can't find a dragon to fight like St George but what about the playground bullies? And can she get over her fear of swimming? Then one day her pet kitten, Halo, goes missing…

Meg Harper combines writing with teaching drama. In her spare time she enjoys swimming, walking her dog, reading and visiting tea shops.

Other titles in this series include:

Saint Jenni: Animal Crazy
Saint Jenni: Chilling Out

For my sister, Janet,
with love

Super Hero

Meg Harper

Illustrations by Jan McCafferty

A Lion Children's Book
an imprint of
Lion Hudson plc
Mayfield House, 256 Banbury Road,
Oxford OX2 7DH, England
www.lionhudson.com
ISBN 0 7459 4895 2

First edition 2004
10 9 8 7 6 5 4 3 2 1 0

A catalogue record for this book is available
from the British Library

Typeset in 13.5/19 Baskerville MT Schoolbook
Printed and bound in Great Britain
by Cox and Wyman Ltd, Reading

Contents

1

Fighting dragons!

'What do you want to be when you grow up?' Miss Simpson asked at school today.

Of course, we all stuck our hands up, until she told us we had to write it down. She said it was because we were going to have lots of visitors, one a week all term, telling us about their jobs. They're the usual suspects – a policeman, a nurse, a builder, a bank manager – they're all someone's mum or dad! We had to think of questions we'd like to ask them too. What good is that to me?

When *I* grow up, I want to be a saint. And I know for a fact that no one's got a saint for a mum or dad – not in this school, anyway. And of course, saints don't go in for having babies much. Far too busy doing daring deeds and suchlike.

'Jenni,' said Miss Simpson, when I'd sat chewing my pencil for five minutes, 'why aren't you writing anything?'

'Can't think of anything to write, Miss.' Writing is not my thing and Miss Simpson knows that perfectly well. She rolled her eyes and tut-tutted in a very unsaintly way.

'Come on now, Jenni. Just have a think what you'd like to be when you grow up,' she said in that fake kind voice teachers use when really they want to scream at you. 'Write it down and that will be a start.'

'You know what I want to be,' I said. 'I want to be a saint.' I had this out with her last term.

'Oh Jenni, you're not *still* on that craze, are you?' she said.

'It's not a craze,' I said stubbornly. 'It's for real.'

Miss Simpson looked at me sadly, almost as if she meant it. 'You know, Jenni,' she said, 'it isn't a very realistic ambition, is it?'

'Why not?'

'Well, hardly anyone gets to be a saint these days. Hardly anyone at all.'

'So? Go and see what Jamie's put. Everyone knows he wants to be an astronaut – and hardly anyone gets to be one of them either. And I bet Daisy has put that she wants to be a ballerina. How many of *them* do you know?'

Miss Simpson glanced round the room. 'You may well be right, Jenni,' she said, 'but there's one big difference between Jamie and Daisy and you.'

'What's that?' I asked suspiciously.

'*They're* managing to write something.'

I glared at Miss Simpson. 'You think I can't write anything about being a saint?' I said. 'You just watch me.'

This is what I wrote:

When I grow up, I want to be a saint. I have been reading about them in my Big Book of

Saints and I have been training hard. Training to be a saint is not easy.

I have discovered that I'm probably not meant to be the sort of saint that does things with animals. I have tried making friends with birds (including penguins), dogs and mice but have not had much success. I do have a very nice kitten called Halo, though. She has a ring of orange fur round one ear so she looks as if she has a halo that's slipped a bit.

One of the problems of training to be a saint is grown-ups who don't understand. My mum and dad do not understand at all and neither does my teacher. When I tried to care for some mice, my mum and dad actually hired a mouse murderer! And when I played pretend saints in the playground, my teacher made me write one hundred lines – even though it was her idea! I guess I should expect this as saints are usually given a very hard time by ignorant people.

The vicar is very nice and helpful and so is our neighbour Mrs Brindley. They both think

that if I want to be a saint I should do more praying but I want to be the sort of saint that does daring deeds. If a dragon comes to this town and I have to fight it, I shall not be sorry if first it eats certain people who don't understand about trainee saints. That may seem like an unsaintly thing to say but I am only a beginner.

As you can see, once I'd got going, there was quite a lot to say but I was still very glad when the bell rang for lunchtime. As soon as I'd had my sandwiches, I ran out with the other girls to practise handstands against the wall. I'm not too sure if trainee saints should show their knickers in public so usually I wear trousers. Today I'd forgotten but I reckon it's the boys staring and calling rude things who are the unsaintly ones really. Drippy Daisy stood there watching.

'I wish I could do handstands,' she said in a feeble voice.

I sighed. Daisy is such a drip she makes the

Niagara Falls look dry but she is useful when no one else wants to play with me. I felt kind of sorry for her.

'Come on, Daisy,' I said. 'I'll stand just here and catch you if you fall.'

'Will you, Jenni?' Her pudgy little cheeks went all pink. Then she hesitated. 'You're not going to let me slip and then laugh at me?'

I put my hands on my hips. 'Daisy, I'm a saint-in-training. Saints don't do mean and horrible.'

'Oh, OK then,' she said, but she still didn't look too sure. She put her hands on the floor (that was a major miracle, she's always so worried about getting dirty) and gave a pathetic little kick with her legs.

'You'll have to do better than that,' I scolded. 'Try again.'

'But people might see my knickers,' she said fretfully.

'So? They've seen mine – doesn't matter.'

Daisy was backing away from me. 'I'll try again tomorrow when I've got my trousers on,' she said.

'Oh come on, Daisy,' I said. 'Don't be such a drip. I may be too busy to help you tomorrow.'

She glanced round to see if anyone was actually looking and then did another of her feeble little kick-offs. Quick as a flash, I grabbed at her legs and flicked her up into a handstand against the wall.

'There you are, Daisy! You've done it!' I said. 'Now try again – but you have to kick harder!'

But Daisy was struggling to get down and I could suddenly see why. Her knickers had Teletubbies on them! They were so old they were saggy. I was flabbergasted. Daisy is so neat and clean, shoes all brightly polished, clothes all carefully ironed, hair in dinky bunches. The tired old knickers were a real shock – she must have had them since she was about three! I dropped her as fast as I could but too late! A bunch of girls was already pointing and giggling.

'Baby Daisy's still got baby knickers!' shouted Jade. 'Has Baby Daisy only just grown out of nappies then?'

'Can't Mummy afford new knickers for Baby Daisy?' sneered Shelley. 'Poor Baby Daisy. Poor, *poor* Baby Daisy.'

Daisy's lip was trembling. 'Don't cry,' I hissed. 'That's what they want! Just don't cry!'

Daisy may be a drip but *no one* should be picked on like that. I wanted to say something very unsaintly indeed to Jade and Shelley. And then I had an inspiration – or that's what I told Miss Simpson afterwards. Standing there all defenceless, Daisy looked just like the princess in the story of St George – which made those bitchy girls into – yes, you've guessed it – the dragon!

I stormed across to them.

'Don't you dare tease Daisy like that! How would you like it? I bet you've got a few old clothes you have to wear sometimes!'

'I have not!' said Jade. 'I'm not poor like she is!'

'And even if I was,' said Shelley, 'I still wouldn't be seen dead in Teletubbies knickers! Teletubbies! What is she like?'

That did it. 'You *will* be dead in a minute,'

I said and before they had time to think, I grabbed both of them by the scruff of their necks and banged their heads together. There was a satisfying clunk and then the bawling started.

'Miss, Miss, she attacked us! Miss, Miss, it hurts!'

'I was just being St George and they were the dragon,' I tried to explain to Miss Simpson, later. 'And you should have heard what they were saying to Daisy.'

'I know,' said Miss Simpson wearily. 'She told me. She said it was her fault and you shouldn't get into trouble.'

'She did?' I was amazed. 'Blimey, she's not such a drip as I thought she was.'

'She's not a drip at all. Daisy has a pretty tough time actually. Anyway, you still shouldn't have done what you did. You are *not* St George and Jade and Shelley are *not* the dragon.'

'No, they're worse,' I agreed. 'They're the biggest bullies in the school.'

'Jenni! That's unfair. A little bit of teasing

doesn't make someone a bully.'

'That's what you think,' I muttered under my breath.

'Jenni, I'm warning you...'

'OK, Miss Simpson,' I said, 'I won't do it again. But they'd better leave Daisy alone, that's all.'

Miss Simpson pulled a strange face. 'Jenni, it wasn't long ago you had to write lines for hitting Daisy. Don't you think you're being a bit two-faced?'

'That was part of a game we were playing,' I tried to explain and then gave up. Miss Simpson would never get it. 'Don't worry, Miss Simpson,' I said, in a soothing voice. 'People never understood the saints in the olden days either.'

Daisy was waiting for me after school. She doesn't live that far from me so she tagged along by my side.

'Thanks for what you did, Jenni,' she said, her pudgy cheeks all pink again. 'I'm sorry you got in trouble.'

'It's OK,' I said gruffly. 'Trouble is good for trainee saints. Thanks for explaining to Miss Simpson.' I was about to leave but Daisy's lip had gone all wobbly and she was redder in the face than ever.

'Oh, don't go and start crying,' I said, in disgust.

Daisy took a deep breath and blinked hard. 'I can't help it about my... well, you know...' she said.

'The Teletubbies?' I said tactfully.

'Yes... you see, I haven't grown very much and so Mum thought it wouldn't matter if I still... I mean, no one's meant to see. And we *haven't* got that much money. She tries ever so hard – she really worries about me looking smart – but...'

'You know what?' I said.

'What?' asked Daisy.

'I think, if they fit, you should wear them. Stuff what everyone else thinks. Waste not, want not. That's what St Margaret said.'

'She did?'

''Course she did. She was very busy looking after poor children and setting up orphanages so she had to.' I crossed my fingers behind my back and hoped God didn't mind the little white lie. I mean, I was sure St Margaret *ought* to have said it.

Daisy beamed at me. 'Well, thanks again, Jenni. I'm really glad you're my friend,' she said and skipped off down her road.

Which made me feel all nice and warm and saintly – for about one minute. It's very saintly to make friends with the people no one else likes... but I think I'd rather fight dragons.

2

Saints don't do stealing

Drippy Daisy and her Teletubbies knickers were really worrying me. I know I said, 'Waste not, want not,' and I meant it – like most of the time the pictures on your pants don't matter – but what else couldn't her mum afford? Could Daisy be so small because she doesn't have enough to eat? I hadn't really thought about it before but she does have free school meals. Maybe there wasn't enough food at home?

I tried getting myself invited back to Daisy's

one night after school.

'How about I come round to play tonight?' I said. 'We could practise handstands. You're getting much better.'

Daisy gave me her frightened-rabbit look. 'Oh no, not tonight,' she said. 'I'd need to ask Mum first.'

'Well, tomorrow night then?'

'Err… well, maybe not this week. Mum's been poorly. Maybe I could come round to yours?'

I wasn't too sure about that. I mean, I was only suggesting we got together after school so that I could suss her home out.

'Well, OK then,' I said reluctantly. 'How about next week we go to yours?'

But there was always some excuse – her mum was too busy, they had to go out, she was too tired – and so it went on. It was quite clear that Daisy didn't want me to go round to her house. She wouldn't even tell me exactly where it was. How bad could it be? I began to imagine an awful, rat-infested hole with broken windows and a leaking roof but it didn't quite fit with Daisy's squeaky-clean clothes. Even so, something was wrong. Teletubbies knickers. *That* was serious.

I was curled up on my bed with Halo snuggling next to me, reading my *Big Book of Saints,* when – bingo! I had my idea! I was reading the story of St Laurence. He was a very brave and daring saint. When Roman soldiers tried to force him into giving them the church treasure, he sneakily sold it and gave the money to the poor people. Then he told them to come to the church as quickly as they could. When the Roman soldiers arrived to collect their loot, the church was full of blind people, disabled people and beggars.

'Here they are!' St Laurence said to the soldiers. 'The true treasures of the church!'

The Romans weren't very impressed with that and dragged him off and killed him – but I bet God was impressed. Dead impressed.

I was sure the vicar who gave me Halo would be impressed too. He cares far more about people than about treasure. He lives just down the road and you should see his house. It's always crawling with children and there isn't a posh thing in sight. And I know he's got a problem with all this stuff called 'the church brasses' because every week it has to be cleaned to keep it bright and shiny. Quite often the people who've said they'll clean it let him down and then he has to do it himself. It's quite good fun, actually, but it takes ages. I sometimes help and so do his kids. We make a bit of a mess but we do make it look like new. Mostly it's candlesticks and plates but there are a couple of crosses too. They're very nice but whenever I help, the vicar always says, 'We could certainly do without doing this last thing on a Friday afternoon.'

My brilliant idea would help Daisy *and* the nice vicar. All I needed to do was sneak into the church and get the brasses! It would be just like St Laurence using the church treasure to help the poor. And it wouldn't be stealing (which would be very unsaintly) because the vicar would be glad to get rid of them. I was sure an antiques shop or even a junk shop would buy them off me – and then

I could give the money to Daisy, or maybe just buy her some new knickers and save them for her birthday. The only problem was getting into the church. It's usually locked. This makes the vicar very sad because he thinks churches should be open for people to go in and pray whenever they want, but these days some people go in to nick stuff.

'Not that there's much worth nicking,' he says. 'Only the blessed church brasses.'

Which seemed like another good reason for getting rid of them.

At first I thought I could just volunteer to take them back to the church one Friday but that would mean waiting for a week when someone forgot to clean them. And I'd look a bit of an obvious suspect too. No, I would have to think of another way – one where there was plenty of time to sell them before anyone noticed that they'd gone. Sunday evening would be a good time. I could sneak in during the evening service, grab all the brasses at the end and then nip out through the side door. You can open it from the inside and it locks itself behind you. We use it to get in and out on a Friday evening.

'I'm just going out rollerblading,' I said to Mum after we'd had our tea the next Sunday.

'OK, love,' she said. 'Just remember to come back the moment it starts getting dark.'

I hesitated for a moment. Yes, I'd be all right. I didn't think the evening service went on very long. There's be plenty of time to get back before dark. I'd hide the brasses in the shed and have a whole week to sell them before anyone noticed they were missing.

Halo watched me pulling on my rollerblades, dabbing at my laces with her paws. She's still only a kitten and investigates absolutely everything. She lay in wait at the front door, ready to dart out. I grabbed her and put her firmly in the sitting room. She follows me everywhere but this time I needed to be alone. I would have welcomed her company though. Now that the moment had come, I was nervous.

St Laurence had to be brave, I told myself firmly. Much braver than you. Come on. Let's get on with it.

I rollerbladed right up to the church and then stopped. Yes, the service had started; I could hear singing. I unfastened my blades and checked that no one was looking. Then I stuffed them under the hedge before tiptoeing into the church in my socks. The church has an entrance hall with loos and cupboards and a kitchen leading off it. I aimed for the little room where all the cleaning stuff is kept. I didn't think anyone would be looking in there that evening.

For a moment, when I turned the handle, I panicked. The door wouldn't budge. Surely it wasn't locked? I tried again and shoved hard with my shoulder. The door shot open with a sudden jolt, catapulting me in and sending the metal mop-bucket clanging into the opposite wall. Quick as a flash, I shoved the door shut and sat down with my back to it, praying that no one had heard. If anyone came to check, with me against the door and the stiff handle, they would think it was locked.

I sat as still as possible, my heart pounding, listening hard. Sure enough, I could hear footsteps in the entrance hall. They paused and then started again, paused and re-started. The handle of my cupboard moved. I almost stopped breathing and leaned all my weight against the door. For a moment, I felt someone's pressure against it, then heard the footsteps again, dying away.

Phew! My breath escaped in a huge sigh. Safe! For now, at least. I waited a few moments, wondering whether to switch on the light. There was no window so it was pitch dark. It would be safe to have the light on for a little while. Later, I would have to turn it off or someone might see it through the crack beneath the door. Stealthily, I reached for the switch and looked around the room. There was a stack of old, oblong cushions in the corner, maybe for people to kneel on when they were praying. Quietly, I piled a few beside the door and sat on them. That was better –

much more comfortable. I'd meant to bring a comic to read but had forgotten. There was nothing for me to do except wait, so I turned off the light in case I forgot later. I sat in the darkness, listening to the murmur of voices from the church. It was warm and stuffy. I yawned. Better not fall asleep, I told myself, and stretched my eyes wide…

I thought I'd only nodded off for a few moments. It had been pitch dark in the cupboard before and it was pitch dark now. But something had changed – something I couldn't quite place for a moment. Then I realized. There was no noise. Absolutely none. The service must have finished – but how long ago?

I shoved the old cushions aside and snatched the door open, expecting daylight on the other side. Instead, the entrance hall was dark – and not the half-dark of twilight. It was night-time now, good and proper.

My heart missed a beat. Mum and Dad!

They'd be going frantic! I had to get home – quickly! But first I must get the brasses. This was my only chance!

I hesitated at the door of the church. Where were the lights? There wasn't time to look. The church has huge windows so there was just about enough light to see. I hurried down the aisle and grabbed a few plates and candlesticks, still with their candles in. I left the crosses; somehow I didn't feel happy about taking them. I piled everything into my big bag and ran for the side door. Only a few minutes and I'd be home. I'd shove the bag under a hedge somewhere and collect it later; there'd be no chance of hiding it in the shed with Mum and Dad watching out for me. They might even have sent for the police!

I tried to turn the knob on the lock. It wouldn't move. Don't panic, I told myself. It's just like the other door. A bit stiff, that's all.

But nothing would shift it. Soon it was slippery with sweat, I was panicking so much. I took some

deep breaths, wiped it with my sleeve and tried again. Nothing.

I gazed around, hoping for a brilliant idea. None came. There was no point in trying the main door. It was bound to be locked. The windows were all high and mostly full of stained glass. They weren't the sort that opened. The windows in the loos were tiny – which left the kitchen.

I sprinted up the aisle with the bag of brasses and burst into the kitchen. My heart sank. All the windows had modern locks. I tested them, just to be sure, but they were well and truly shut.

'What am I going to do?' I howled. It wasn't the idea of staying the night in the church that was freaking me out, it was the thought of Mum and Dad going mad with worry. They were bound to get the police soon, if they hadn't already. For all I knew, it might be midnight. Who would ever think of looking in the church? There'd be banner headlines in the papers and heart-rending news broadcasts, my mum sobbing into a microphone while I quietly starved to death in the church. I'd chosen tonight so it would be days before the missing brasses were noticed. I might be stuck all week!

That was when I really panicked. I ran to the main doors and hammered on them, shouting at the top of my voice. Surely someone would see or hear me? Surely someone might be passing even if it was really late? Someone walking their dog perhaps? Or the police if they were looking for me?

But the church is set back from the road. I could hardly even see the gate. No one would be able to see me.

'Aagh!' I screamed. 'What am I going to do? If you're really there, God, give me an idea!'

And he did! Well, you *could* put it down to coincidence – my dad certainly did – but the next moment, I knew what to do. Calmly, I started looking for the light switches. They weren't difficult to find – just inside the church on the wall on the right. I had to pile up a few of those old cushions to reach them but that didn't take long. Then I started signalling. Lights on, lights off, lights on, lights off. Surely someone would see and come to investigate, even if they weren't looking for me?

It didn't take long. It was the vicar who came to the rescue. I heard him unlocking the door and rushed to meet him, flinging my arms round him I was so relieved.

'Jenni!' he cried. 'What on earth are *you* doing stuck in here?'

'I was trying to steal the church brasses,' I sobbed. 'Like St Laurence!'

'But why?' he gasped.

'So I could buy some new knickers for Daisy!'

He looked at me like I was stark, staring bonkers and I could certainly see why.

'Come on, Jenni,' he said. 'I think we'd better get you home.'

3

Can saints walk on water?

How was I to know that the side door to the church had a special lock? If it's locked from the outside, it *won't* open from the inside. So that was why I couldn't get out. And how was I to know that if the vicar gets rid of the church brasses, loads of people will be upset? I mean, he never says that when he's got to clean them. And if they care that much, why can't they remember to clean them themselves?

The vicar explained all this to me as we hurried

home. He also explained that St Laurence had been *in charge* of the church treasure – him selling it and me taking the brasses weren't really the same at all. I began to feel pretty stupid. I felt even more stupid when, just my luck, we found a police car parked outside my house.

'Ah,' said the vicar. 'I don't think we'd better say you got locked in the church because you were trying to take the brasses. Let's think quickly. What's your story?'

'Saints don't do lying,' I said firmly. 'And neither should vicars.'

'Not even little white lies?'

'W…e…ll,' I said slowly, thinking of some I'd told in the past. 'No… no… I think it's far better to stick to the truth. Far more saintly.'

'I see,' said the vicar and sighed. 'Well, then, on your own halo be it.'

We marched up to our front door – well, that is, the vicar marched and I kind of slunk. Now that there was only a door between me and the police, I wasn't feeling quite so saintly.

The vicar rang the bell. The next moment, it was flung open by my mum.

'Jenni!' she cried. 'Where on earth have you been?' She pulled me against her and nearly smothered me with kisses.

'She's been in the church,' said the vicar, following us in. 'She got locked in by mistake.'

A policeman and a policewoman were in our small sitting room. They seemed to almost fill it.

'Well, then,' said the policeman, standing up. 'All's well that ends well. Just a couple of questions before we go, Jenni. How did you come to be locked in the church?'

'I… I… I…' Suddenly, I felt very scared and very stupid but I still couldn't lie. Not after what I'd said to the vicar. 'I was trying to take the church brasses,' I gabbled. 'I was going to sell them to get some money for my friend who is very poor.'

I'm sure police hear some surprising things in their job, but I don't think either of them had heard that one before. They stood there speechless, gaping at me.

‘Jenni!’ said Mum. ‘How could you? The vicar is your friend!’

‘I can explain that,’ said the vicar. ‘She thought I wanted to get rid of the brasses.’

‘So this is true?’ said the policewoman. ‘You can confirm it.’

‘Oh yes,’ said the vicar. ‘I went to the church because the lights were flashing on and off and there was Jenni with the church brasses all packed up in a swag-bag.’

There was a stunned silence.

‘Err… don’t worry,’ said the vicar. ‘I’m not going to press charges. Just a bit of a misunderstanding about Christian charity, that’s all. I’m sure Jenni isn’t really a thief.’

‘Right,’ said the policeman, still looking as though he’d been slapped round the face with a wet fish. ‘We’d better be on our way. So, Miss, no more stealing the church brasses, eh? Is that clear?’

I nodded my head furiously. I just wanted them all to go away so that I could run up to my bedroom, shove my head under my pillow and cry.

My mum saw the police out.

'Well, Jenni,' she said, when she came back. 'I really don't know where to start. Your dad and I have been so worried – and all the time, you've been trying to steal from the church! Haven't we taught you the difference between right and wrong? And look, you've really upset the vicar too!'

The vicar had sat down on the sofa, mopping his eyes with his hankie. His shoulders were shaking.

'Oh no, really...' he said. 'I'm not upset. I'm sorry... I shouldn't be laughing... you've been so worried. But the look on that policeman's face! You were quite right, Jenni – it was far better to tell the truth!'

At that my dad, who had looked ready to burst since the moment I got home, started to laugh too. 'I have been *so* worried, Jenni,' he said. 'And then I was *so* angry. But the vicar is right. There really is a funny side too.'

'Well, I'm glad you think so,' said my mum, looking ready to slap the two men laughing helplessly on the sofa, 'because I don't! And if you pull another stunt like that, Jenni, you won't be going out to play after tea ever again! I've never heard anything so outrageous! Now off you go to bed. You've got school in the morning.'

I hurried up the stairs. I don't think I've ever been so glad to be sent to bed.

The next morning, I woke up feeling tired and grumpy. It had been late by the time I got to bed and just when I was beginning to fall asleep, Mum came to have a serious chat with me about stealing, staying out after dark and getting locked in churches. She was wasting her time! Think I want to try any of them again? You've got to be joking! And I still hadn't solved the problem of Daisy's Teletubbies knickers. I just hoped she'd have the sense to wear a different pair because today we were starting swimming at school.

Urgh! That *was* something to be grumpy about. Every year, we get about half a term of swimming lessons down at the local pool. I hate it. Even though we only get about twenty minutes in the water by the time we've got there and mucked about in the changing rooms. I know it's a bit feeble if you want to be the sort of saint who does daring deeds – but I'm frightened of water.

I don't think I'm called to be a saint like St Patrick who seemed to be forever crossing the sea to Ireland or St Paul who made a habit of surviving shipwrecks. As for St Cuthbert who prayed all night, standing in the sea – well, forget it! The very thought gives me the heebie-jeebies! And just don't mention St Christopher! Carrying children across rivers in flood! I'd rather be burnt at the stake like Joan of Arc! Lots of saints were! Actually, on second thoughts, I'd rather not do that either. That's what's so amazing about saints – they believed in God so strongly, they just wouldn't give up their faith even if they were tortured and killed. Lucky for me that there are laws against it in this country. I can be the sort of saint who dies peacefully in her bed – after I've done some daring deeds of course.

Both Mum and Dad have tried really hard to

teach me to swim. Mum kept taking me to the toddler pool when I was little, even though I screamed so loudly that I'm surprised she wasn't reported for cruelty. And every so often, Dad gets this glint in his eye and says, 'Come on, Jenni! Let's have another bash at swimming!' Off we trek to the pool, even though we know it's useless. We watch all the other kids messing about on the flumes and the floats and my blood runs cold. I can force myself into the water now, but that's about it. A few strokes and I start to panic, even with armbands and a float. And I'm getting a bit old for armbands now. They make me feel like a complete idiot.

Daisy's not great at swimming either but at least she's not scared. Standing on the side shivering, watching her bobbing about, I wonder how I dare to call her a drip.

Jade and Shelley are brilliant at swimming. They've been having lessons for years and now they're in the swimming club – but they've never had a go at me about it before. I guess that's what you get for bashing people's heads together.

I was waiting by the pool, feeling very silly in my armbands, dreading the moment when the teacher told us to get in. Jade and Shelley strolled past, making for the deep end. We're split into groups for swimming and they're in the top group, of course.

It was Daisy that they sneered at first.

'I'm surprised you haven't got Barbie on your swimsuit,' said Shelley. 'Did Baby Daisy grow out of that one then?'

'She never had one,' said Jade. 'She can't afford to go swimming.'

I nearly shoved her in the pool! But I was too scared. I simply couldn't risk slipping and falling in myself.

Jade laughed. 'St Jenni isn't much good to you today, is she?' she taunted. 'She's too scared of the water to come to your rescue!'

It wasn't much – maybe she remembered how much her head had hurt – but it stung. Nobody has teased me for wanting to be a saint before, apart from my dad.

Right, I told myself. This is it. You can't be scared of the water any more. Saints have to be brave and bold. They can't go round snivelling about getting water up their noses!

It was easier said than done. I inched closer to the edge of the pool and my knees nearly buckled. I stepped back again. If only the teacher would let us get into the water! It was worse standing there looking at it than being in it! But because it was the first lesson of the term, the teacher was going on and on about safety and what we could do and what we couldn't! At this rate, there wouldn't be time to swim at all.

I was beginning to feel queasy. 'Please, please let us get in the water!' I said under my breath. If I had to stand there much longer, I'd be sick. It had happened once before with Mum. And then what would Jade and Shelley say?

I tried to take my mind off it, checking off all the brave saints I could think of. I grinned to myself when I got to St Peter. I think he's my favourite saint. He was always speaking out bravely – and putting his foot in it! And then I remembered! He was the one who walked on water – but he panicked and Jesus had to save him. Well, if Jesus could help St Peter walk on water in a storm – before he was a saint, as well – then he could jolly well help me swim in a swimming pool!

I didn't hesitate. Something had to happen or my breakfast would reappear. I walked boldly forwards and stepped straight into the pool!

The next moment, everything was a thrashing blur of turquoise blue. A long way away, I could hear people calling but there was a strange fuzzy roaring in my ears. I didn't wait to hit the bottom but struck out with my arms, trying to blow bubbles like the teacher had made us do with our faces in the water. I kicked out with my legs too. I had to do it. I had to swim. It had to be now – or Jade and Shelley would laugh at me forever.

My face burst out of the water. I couldn't have been under for more than a few seconds but it was enough for me. I had done what had always

terrified me and I was still alive! It could never be so bad again. I was snorting and choking but my arms and legs seemed to have taken on a life of their own. They were forcing me towards the other side of the pool. My lungs were bursting but then I remembered that you had to breathe like a goldfish.

'Jenni, you're swimming! Come on, Jenni! You can do it! Keep going Jenni!' It was Daisy, running along the edge of the pool in her excitement. Everyone else seemed to be shouting too but it was Daisy I could hear, shrieking above the hubbub.

When my hands touched the opposite wall, I thought I would faint for joy. I didn't think even St Peter could have felt so fantastic when Jesus helped him walk to the boat.

'Jenni Gardner!' the teacher shouted. I turned and looked at her and nearly laughed. Her tracksuit bottoms were round her ankles. Then I realized what that meant. She had thought I was drowning and had been about to plunge in after me. 'Get out of the pool immediately!' she shrieked.

It was only a few metres to the steps but I swam. I swam! And I didn't care what the teacher was going to say or how much trouble I was going to get into. I could swim! I had never been so pleased with myself, never in my entire life!

4

A disastrous game

I was so thrilled by my triumph at the swimming pool that I'm afraid Daisy's knicker problem began to fade into the background. Daisy seemed happy enough though. Dad was as excited as I was about the swimming and for weeks we went every Saturday. We started taking Daisy too because, once I got confident, Dad liked to go off and do a few lengths on his own and it was far more fun if I'd got Daisy to play with.

It's a funny thing about Daisy. She's so prissy

about some things but get her in the swimming pool and she's wild. When we go on the flumes, she's always thinking of different ways to slide down. Once she got told off by the lifeguard but it didn't bother her at all. I'd have been shaking. Anyway, as the weeks went by, I was very pleased to notice that the knicker issue was solved. Daisy's mum must have got her some new ones. The dreaded Teletubbies were never seen again – so maybe she wasn't as hard up as I'd thought she was.

It made me glad I was going to be a saint that does daring deeds rather than the sort who gives all her money to the poor. Selling the church brasses to raise money for Daisy was one thing but I didn't fancy going round wearing rags. Just think what Jade and Shelley would say about that. Urgh! I know people tell you that sticks and stones may break your bones and words can never hurt you but it's a load of old rubbish. I'd prefer the sticks and stones myself – at least bruises get better. You can't forget words.

What did I say about bruises? I must have

been mad! God must have decided to set me a saintliness test. I'm here, lying on the sofa cuddling Halo, with a huge bandage wrapped round my head and it's the first time in days that I haven't woken up with a headache! Nothing has ever hurt so much in my whole life. How did the old saints put up with all that pain? D'you know that there was a saint called Rose of Lima who deliberately wore gloves full of nettles and slept on piles of bricks? And she wore a crown of roses, not to make her look nice but so that all the thorns dug in! She thought this would make up for all the thoughtless, sinful people who didn't care about God! She must have been bonkers! OK, so I know some saints came to some very sticky ends – St Stephen for one – but choosing to sleep on bricks! I'm not sure that's very saintly at all! It better not be, anyway, or I'll have to be something else instead!

Anyway, this is what happened to my head. Don't laugh – it isn't funny.

Daisy and I have been getting a bit bored with

doing handstands at playtimes at school. Now that we can both do them really well – I can even walk on my hands for a few steps – it isn't much fun. We tried learning how to do cartwheels too but the dinner-ladies won't let us – they say they're too dangerous! Huh! Would I have ended up with stitches in my head if I'd done a few cartwheels? I don't think so – and when I get back to school I'm jolly well going to tell the dinner-ladies! You have to stand up for what you believe in if you're a saint – and I believe in cartwheels for kids!

The point is, if we'd been allowed to do cartwheels, we wouldn't have been playing 'saints'– and that was where the trouble started. The last time we played 'saints',* Daisy was really pathetic about it. She wouldn't do a thing and I ended up hitting her and getting lines to write – so when she suggested it, I thought maybe I was hearing voices in my head, like Joan of Arc.

'Did you say something, Daisy?' I asked suspiciously.

* *See Saint Jenni: Animal Crazy*

'Yes. I said, 'Let's play "saints". We haven't played that for ages.'

'But you didn't like it last time we played.'

'Only 'cos you kept bossing me about. But you're not as bossy as you used to be.'

'That's because you're not such a drip.'

'I'm not a drip at all,' said Daisy fiercely.

I nearly laughed. Daisy is small and blonde with round, pink cheeks. When she tries to look fierce, she just looks like a mildly grumpy guinea pig.

'Anyway,' she continued. 'I want to play St Stephen or St Paul. Or maybe St Sebastian.'

'Urgh!' I said. 'Some pretty horrible things happened to them.'

'But they're exciting!' said Daisy, stamping her foot. 'I don't want to play about nice, kind saints who shared their sandwiches with rabbits!'

'No, no,' I said. 'You're thinking of St Sergius. He shared his bread with a bear!'

'Doesn't matter. He didn't get eaten, did he? He didn't even have to fight the bear! Where's the fun in that?'

'Well, OK, then,' I said uncertainly, 'but you won't have to mind if you get your hands dirty or something.'

'Why should I get my hands dirty?' Daisy demanded. 'I'm not really going to burn you at the stake!'

That was a relief. The way Daisy was carrying on, I wouldn't have been surprised if she'd suddenly produced some matches and started building a bonfire! Pretending sounded far too dull for her!

'Right then,' I said. 'Let's start with St Sebastian. That's quite an exciting one. He won't give up his faith so the soldiers use him for target practice with their bows and arrows. Then, when they think he's dead, an old lady rescues him and nurses him back to health. You stand over there and be St Sebastian.'

Daisy went along with this happily. She seemed to really enjoy the bit where I pretended to shoot arrows at her and she had to writhe about in agony. She's certainly a lot more fun to play with than she used to be. We did it a couple of times. The second time, we made darts out of some old paper I had in my bag so that it was a bit more realistic – but then one of the dinner-ladies came stomping over and told us off for making a mess.

'Let's do someone else then,' said Daisy when she'd gone. 'Let's do St Stephen.'

'OK,' I said. 'I'll be the crowd of people who don't believe in Jesus and you do the bit where St Stephen tells them how it's their fault he was crucified.'

'No,' said Daisy. 'You be St Stephen. I'll be the crowd.'

'But I want to be…' I started.

'I was St Sebastian,' Daisy argued. 'It's your turn to be the saint. And you're better at making speeches than me.'

'But…' I didn't like this. 'Saints' was my game and I didn't want Daisy taking over.

Daisy pouted at me. 'If you don't do it my way, I'm not playing with you any more,' she said.

'Huh!' I said. 'No one else is going to play with *you!*'

'I'll go and do handstands,' she said. 'I don't mind. I'm good at them now.'

I thought about it. It was certainly more fun playing 'saints' than doing handstands or wandering round the playground on my own.

'That's not fair,' I objected. 'It was me that showed you how to do handstands.'

'And it was me that showed you how to dive.'

I didn't think that had anything to do with it, even though it was true, and I said so.

'All right, be like that,' she said and ran off towards the girls doing handstands.

I stood there with my hands in my pockets, not sure what to do. Lunchtime was nowhere near over and I certainly wasn't going to just give in. In the end, I sauntered over, trying to look cool. Saints have to try to be kind and think of others before themselves but it's a struggle, I can tell you.

'I'll be St Stephen as long as you're Rose of Lima when we play tomorrow,' I said cunningly.

'Rose of Lima? She sounds nice. What does she have to do?'

'Oh, nothing much. Mostly just look beautiful.' Daisy looked unsure. 'But it's a very exciting story,' I added quickly. She could find out about the gloves full of nettles later. Then she'd know who was the boss around here.

I quite enjoyed delivering St Stephen's speech. I wasn't quite sure what I was supposed to say but it certainly made Daisy look pretty scared.

'That's enough,' she shouted suddenly. 'You are a terrible blabberer and must be put to death. Take him away and stone him!'

'It's blasphemer not blabberer,' I said scornfully. 'It means saying bad things about God.'

'Well, I think you're a blabberer, so there!' said Daisy. 'Blab, blab, blab. You go on forever. Now stand over there while I stone you.'

I glowered at her but went and stood by the wall where she told me to. I'd get my own back the next day. I could make a nice, prickly crown of roses before then.

That's when everything went pear-shaped. I thought Daisy would just pretend to throw things at me but, suddenly, she picked something up from the floor. It was about the right size and shape for a stone. She threw it hard.

'No, Daisy!' I shouted, holding up my arm to protect myself. I ducked awkwardly, fell over my own feet, and went headlong into the wall. There was a blinding flash of light and then nothing – not even pain.

'Jenni, Jenni, are you all right?' The voice was familiar but I couldn't quite place it.

'She's dead, oh I've killed her, oh no, oh what am I going to do?'

I knew who that was. It was Daisy, crying hysterically – but why? Was I dead? Surely your head wouldn't hurt so much if you were dead? I remembered the flash of light. Maybe something had happened to me like St Paul. He was blinded by a bright light on the road to Damascus. Was I blind, then? Slowly, painfully, I opened my eyes and tried to focus. A whole crowd of kids was staring at me and my teacher, Miss Simpson, was gazing down at me anxiously.

'Oh thank goodness,' she said. 'She's coming round.'

'Does that mean I haven't killed her?' Daisy snivelled.

'Of course you haven't killed her,' Miss Simpson snapped. 'She just fell and knocked herself out. But that's a very nasty gash she's got on her head. She's going to have to go to hospital.'

'She *did* try to kill me,' I said. 'She threw a stone at me.'

'No I didn't!' said Daisy. 'I wouldn't have thrown a real stone at you, Jenni. It was only my apple!'

'Never mind that now, Daisy,' said Miss Simpson. 'It doesn't matter how it happened. Pull yourself together and go and ask for the first-aid box, please. We need something to stop the bleeding. And tell Mrs Stewart to ring for Jenni's Mum or Dad to come and get her.'

And so I was packed off to hospital and stitched

up. It took them half an hour to pick out all the bits of dirt and grit with some extra-long tweezers. It was torture. It made me think about St Catherine. D'you know what the emperor was going to do to her? Just because she wouldn't worship the old Roman gods? Tie her round a wheel with spikes sticking out and roll her down a hill! Urgh! Fortunately, all the spikes fell off in a blaze of light – so they chopped her head off instead! Anyway, I had to stay in hospital overnight because they thought I might have concussion. It was horrible. I kept drifting off to sleep and then waking up not knowing where I was, with my head throbbing away. I almost wished *my* head had been cut off! I swore revenge on Daisy there and then. After all I'd done for her – standing up for her against Jade and Shelley, teaching her handstands, taking her swimming, even trying to steal for her! If she'd been St Stephen like I wanted, this would never have happened.

Mrs Brindley from next door but one came to see me with some chocolates so I told her all about it. She's got four big kids and is very kind so I thought she'd understand. She didn't.

'Jenni, love, we all make mistakes. Daisy didn't mean to hurt you. It was only an apple she threw. She must feel dreadful. Has she been round to see you?'

'Yes,' I snarled.

'And did she say sorry?'

'No. I told Mum I didn't want to see her. And I don't. I'm never going to speak to her again.'

Mrs Brindley smiled but in a sad sort of way. 'Oh dear, Jenni,' she said. 'I thought you wanted to be a saint. Saints have to be very forgiving, you know.'

I rolled over on the sofa so I couldn't see her. 'My head's hurting again,' I said, and she went away.

Well, I don't care what Mrs Brindley says, I'm not speaking to Daisy ever again. I shall take a vow of silence against her. That's a pretty saintly thing to do, I'm sure. God will just have to make do with that.

5

Two loose teeth

I'm keeping my promise. When saints made a vow, they stuck with it. I went back to school today but I didn't speak to Daisy. She came running up to me in the playground when I got there, like a little puppy that's been naughty and is trying to get back in your good books.

'Oh, Jenni,' she said. 'I'm so glad you're better. I called round but your mum said you weren't feeling well. And then my mum was poorly this week so I haven't been able to come again.'

Her eyes were all melty and full of tears. Pathetic! She really is such a drip. She did this great big snort of a snivel and said, 'Jenni, I'm so sorry about what happened. I really didn't mean to hurt you, honest.'

I glared at her and turned on my heel. If she didn't mean to hurt me, why throw an apple at me? I mean, that would have hurt if it had hit me, wouldn't it? She was stupid as well as a drip!

She ran after me. 'Jenni, you're not still mad at me, are you? You are still my friend? I just got kind of carried away with the game!' She was beginning to cry properly now.

I walked away quickly. My head was beginning to ache. She was such a pain. I'd put up with her long enough. She'd have to find another friend – if she could. There were plenty of kids who'd play with *me*. I'd manage fine.

But right then, I didn't feel like playing or speaking to anyone. I was far too grumpy. It was cold and the wind was making my cut hurt and my eyes smart. I blew my nose hard and that made my head throb again. I couldn't wait for the whistle to blow for us to line up. I sat on a low wall and waited. And that was when I noticed my wobbly tooth. It was a big one. Most of the easy front ones had already fallen out. I prodded at it with my tongue. Yes, definitely loose. I worked at it, the way you do. Once you've got a wobbly tooth, your tongue can't seem to leave it alone. It kept me busy till it was time to go inside.

Playtime wasn't much fun either. My head stopped me from doing handstands and I wasn't speaking to Daisy, of course. I didn't feel too good anyway. I sat on the wall, poked at my tooth and wished I was still at home. At lunchtime, Miss Simpson let me stay inside with a book. She thought I was looking a bit pale.

I *felt* a bit pale. By the end of the day, I'd prodded my tooth so much that it really hurt and the occasional throbbing in my head had become a steady ache. Mum sent me to bed early, and in the morning my head felt much better. Not my tooth though. It was really sore. Dad laughed when I refused my toast because of it.

'What a fuss about a loose tooth!' he said. 'They don't hurt!'

'This one does,' I protested.

'Well, if it's not fallen out by tonight, I'll tie a bit of thread to it and yank it out for you. That's what my dad always did. Gets it over with quicker. You'll be back to eating toast in no time.'

'Jeff!' said my mum. 'Not while we're having breakfast, please!'

'You're a couple of wimps!' he said. 'It's by far the best thing to do. Come to think of it, Jenni, there was some saint or other who had her teeth pulled out. Had a funny name – Apollo or something. Now where did I hear about her? Anyway, it just goes to show that beginner saints ought to have their teeth pulled out. It's good practice for later. I'll do it tonight, then, shall I, Jenni?' He ruffled my hair jovially.

'Get off, Dad,' I said grumpily. 'You're hurting my head. And there certainly isn't any St Apollo in *my* book of saints.'

'Oh lighten up, Jenni,' he said, 'I'm sure there is one. Ask at school.' And with that he bounced off to work.

Urgh! Parents! St Clare had to run away from hers because they were trying to force her into marrying someone she couldn't stand. I suppose I ought to be glad that mine aren't that bad!

Anyway, it was another miserable day at school. Daisy had given up trying to speak to me but I wouldn't have wanted to play anyway. My head wasn't so bad but now my gum was throbbing all down one side. My tongue simply wouldn't leave my tooth alone, even though it hurt.

When I got home, I burst into tears.

'Oh dear, Jenni,' said Mum. 'Maybe your dad's right and he should pull your tooth out. I'd rather let nature take its course myself, but it does seem to be giving you a lot of trouble. You'd better have some medicine.'

'I'm not letting Dad anywhere near it,' I said. 'I don't trust him. And he'd laugh.'

Mum put her arm round me. 'Did you find out

about that saint he was on about? Fancy your dad knowing about one you hadn't heard of!'

I'd forgotten about that. I was annoyed. I'd meant to find out so that I could put Dad in his place.

'I'll look on the Internet,' I said.

Mum shrugged. 'It's worth a try,' she said.

It's amazing what you can find out on the Internet. It took me a while but I got there in the end. I found a website all about patron saints and there she was – not Apollo but Apollonia, the patron saint of dentists. There wasn't much about her, but she'd certainly been tortured for her faith in God by having her teeth pulled out. In some versions of the story they miraculously grew back again! Amazing!

I went and told Mum. 'D'you think it'd be very painful?' I asked.

'What? Having all your teeth pulled out? I should jolly well think it would!'

'No, just pulling this one out. It really hurts – I just want to get rid of it.'

Mum looked at me. 'And you don't want your dad to do it?'

'No way.'

'Hmm…' Mum looked unsure. 'I'm a bit squeamish about that sort of thing… but I do remember my brothers doing it. I think I could manage.'

'What did they do?'

'Well, they'd fasten a piece of thread to the wobbly tooth and then tie the end to the door handle. Then the one with the loose tooth would hang onto the end of the bed or something – and the other one would go and slam the door shut. Worked every time.'

I thought about it. It couldn't be that bad. St Apollonia had all her teeth pulled out when they weren't even loose and she'd survived.

'Want to try?' asked Mum.

'Where do you keep the thread?' I said.

We didn't tell Dad when he got home. We just put the tooth under his tumbler at the tea table. The glass kind of magnified it. It looked really gruesome. For a moment, we thought he wouldn't notice but then…

'Aagh! What's that?' he exclaimed. 'What's under my glass?' He leapt up in alarm.

Mum and I fell about laughing.

'You great wimp!' said Mum. 'It's only Jenni's tooth. Honestly! What are you like?'

Dad took a deep breath and sat down. 'Well, I wasn't expecting it,' he blustered. 'It's not often we have teeth on the menu.' He smiled bravely. 'So it fell out then did it, Jenni?'

'No,' I said smugly. 'I found out about St Apollonia. They tortured her by pulling all her teeth out. So I thought, if she could do it, so could I. And then I pulled it out. No sweat.'

'On your own?'

'Well, Mum helped a bit.'

'I don't believe it! She's so squeamish she had to ring me to take you to the hospital the other day! How did you do it?'

'Ha!' said Mum. 'Who was it fainted when

Jenni's room got over-run with mice?'*

'That's got nothing to do with it. Tell me how you pulled her tooth out!'

'Shan't,' said Mum and folded her arms, 'but don't laugh at people with toothache or we might come and pull yours out in the night!'

It was a couple of weeks later that I came upon Jade and Shelley hiding in the school loos. Jade had her arm round Shelley who was crying. I didn't think either of them had a soft bone in their body, so it was a real shock.

'What's up?' I blurted before I could stop myself. 'If you stay here you'll get in trouble.'

'We know that, stupid,' said Jade, 'but it's really cold and Shelley doesn't want to go outside.'

'Why not?'

'Because she's got toothache, nosy,' said Jade. 'OK?'

'Why doesn't she tell Miss Simpson? Maybe she can give her something for it.'

'Because, Little Miss Fix-It, it's a wobbly tooth.

* *See Saint Jenni: Animal Crazy*

Miss Simpson'll tell her to stop making such a fuss – wobbly teeth don't hurt.'

'Huh! That's what my dad said to me but mine was agony. In the end, I pulled it out. It was such a relief.'

'You pulled it out? On your own?' Jade looked amazed. 'How?'

'Well, my mum helped a bit. It was easy.' Quickly, I explained what we had done. 'I could do it for Shelley if she wants me to.' I don't like Shelley. In fact, I was quite enjoying watching her sobbing – she's made so many little girls miserable, she deserves to cry a whole ocean herself. But enjoying watching people weep is not a saintly thing to do. Making them better is – so I thought at least I ought to offer.

'What d'you think, Shelley?' asked Jade.

Shelley lifted her tear-stained face. 'Could you do it now?'

'If we're quick,' I said. 'I'd have to get a piece of thread from somewhere.'

'Will it hurt a lot?' asked Shelley.

'Only for a second,' I assured her.

Jade and Shelley looked at one another. 'Let's do it,' said Shelley.

'There's some thread in Miss Simpson's desk,' said Jade. 'With the sticky tape and the drawing pins and everything. One of us'll have to sneak in and get it.' She was looking at me.

'No sweat,' I said with a gulp. We're not allowed in the classroom at lunchtime unless we have special permission, and I certainly didn't want to be caught rooting in Miss Simpson's desk. But compared with fighting dragons and being burnt alive it was a doddle – so I thought I'd better get on with it.

'I'll stand guard,' said Jade which is the first helpful thing she's ever said to me. I reckoned my saintly behaviour was having quite a good effect.

We sneaked out of the loos and back to the classroom. No one was around so I bolted straight in. It took only seconds to find the thread but I could barely pick it up, my hands were shaking so much. Suddenly, Jade started waving at me frantically. Did she mean I should get out or hide? I didn't fancy getting caught in the classroom so I ran for it.

'Phew!' gasped Jade when I burst into the corridor. 'Miss Simpson was just at the end there – but she went off in the other direction. Sorry if I scared you.'

'It's OK,' I said. I was beginning to enjoy myself. Jade could be quite good fun if she weren't so bitchy.

We hurried back to the loos. Shelley was peering at her tooth in the mirror. 'It's quite a big one,' she said anxiously.

She was right. It was a whopper. Suddenly, I had a bad feeling about this – but I couldn't back out now.

'Quick!' I said. 'Let's just do it.'

I was all fingers and thumbs but somehow managed to make a loop in the thread like Mum had done and tighten it round Shelley's tooth. Then I fastened the other end round a cubicle doorknob.

'OK,' I said, checking to see that the thread

was the right length. 'Hold onto the washbasin really tightly.'

Shelley did as she was told.

'You're sure this will be all right?' said Jade anxiously.

''Course,' I said and, before Shelley could change her mind, I slammed the door shut hard.

'Aagh!' screamed Shelley as – ping! – her tooth shot across the room. 'Aagh! Aagh! Aagh!'

'Oh, don't make such a fuss,' I said. 'It's done now.'

Just then, the door of the loos flew open and Miss Simpson strode in.

'Girls!' she said. 'What on earth is going on in here? What was that dreadful noise?'

Shelley was sobbing fit to burst.

'Whatever's the matter, Shelley?' demanded Miss Simpson. 'Take your hand away from your mouth and tell me!'

Shelley did as she was told and, honestly, I have never seen so much blood. Her mouth seemed to be full of it and it was dripping down her wrist. I stood there, petrified. What had I done? Pulled her tongue out by mistake?

Jade had gone all white and shaky. She lifted a trembling arm and pointed straight at me.

'It was her,' she said loudly. 'She did it. It's all Jenni's fault, Miss, honest.'

The skunk! I couldn't believe it. I felt just like Joan of Arc must have done – one minute everyone likes you and you're a heroine, the next minute they're burning you at the stake.

'Jenni,' said Miss Simpson. 'Go straight to the Headmistress's office and wait outside. When we've sorted out poor Shelley, I think you have some explaining to do.'

'But…' I started.

'Just go!' thundered Miss Simpson.

Honestly! Talk about unfair! I try to be brave and bold and daring and *nobody* appreciates it! Absolutely no one! I'll never make it to being a saint at this rate. How *did* the old saints cope?

6

St Jenni – super hero?

The Headmistress was more understanding than Miss Simpson. It turned out she knows about saints.

'Well, Jenni,' she said. 'Why don't you tell me what happened? I imagine there's quite a simple explanation really.'

As clearly as I could, I explained. I must admit, it did get a bit confused, especially when I couldn't remember St Apollonia's name. But the Headmistress could.

'Ah, St Apollonia,' she said. 'The patron saint of dentists.'

'You know about her?' I said, amazed.

The Headmistress nodded. 'We celebrate a lot of saints' days in my church,' she said. 'I agree with you – they're fascinating. But I've never heard of anyone *training* to be a saint. It seems to me it's more about listening to God and doing what he tells you than practising doing saintly things.'

'But lots of saints spent years and years being nuns or monks,' I argued. 'That's training to be a saint! Some of them were really young when they started! St Thérèse was only fifteen when she became a nun!'

'And the main thing she's remembered for is believing that anyone can serve God by doing everyday things in a spirit of kindness,' said the Headmistress.

'Well, I was *trying* to be kind,' I said. 'Shelley's really mean but I still helped her pull her tooth out. I didn't know it was going to bleed so much!'

I had a suspicion that the Headmistress was

trying not to smile. 'It's not very kind to say she's really mean though, is it?' she said.

I glowered at her. 'But she is,' I said.

'Jenni, I'm not going to say anything more about this,' said the Headmistress. 'I can see you were trying to be kind and it went wrong. But I do have a bit of advice for you. Saints do lots of talking and listening to God. I think that's what you should be practising.'

'You mean praying?' I said.

'Yes.'

'That's just what Mrs Brindley our neighbour says.'

'And have you tried?'

'Sometimes. But it gets a bit boring.'

The Headmistress smiled. 'Yes, it can,' she said, 'but a bit of boredom's probably less painful than having all your teeth pulled out. Now off you go.'

It took me a while to work out what she was on about. I guess she means that if you can't put up with a bit of praying, then you're not going to be able to put up with something nasty like being tortured. I don't know – grown-ups! They do make everything so dull! Can't you be a daring-deeds saint without doing the praying? I don't see why not.

Maybe I do see now. Well, a bit better than I did. Just maybe.

It had been raining all week. Not feeble bits of drizzle, but real rain coming down like stair-rods. Halo, my kitten, was very fed up. She hates getting wet but she hates staying in all the time too. When I got home from school, I couldn't find her anywhere.

'Have you seen Halo?' I asked Mum.

'No, I haven't seen her for hours,' she said. 'Isn't she curled up somewhere?'

'I've looked everywhere.'

'Well, she's probably out then. She'll be back when she's hungry.'

'Mum! It's pouring with rain. She wouldn't stay out long in this! I'll have to go and look for her!'

'Don't be silly, darling,' said Mum. 'She's

probably just asleep somewhere. Look round the house again.'

My stomach was churning horribly. What if something dreadful had happened to Halo?

'I've looked!' I shouted. 'She's not here. She might have been hit by a car, she might be stuck up a tree, she might have drowned somewhere, she might be freezing…'

'Jenni, stop panicking,' said Mum. 'Wait until teatime. I'm sure she'll appear then.'

'But by then it'll be dark!'

'Jenni, go and watch the telly to take your mind off it. One thing's for sure, you're not going out again now. Just look at that rain!'

Well, I wasn't going to put up with that. I just had to go and look for Halo. I said nothing and walked obediently into the sitting room as if I was going to do as I was told. Then, when I thought Mum had forgotten about me, I sneaked out of the front door. St Jenni, Super Hero, off on a rescue mission, that was me – except I didn't feel at all heroic, just sad and worried.

The rain wasn't so bad now. If I hurried, I could have a good look round the churchyard and the park before it got dark. I hoped I wouldn't meet the vicar at the church. I had a suspicion he'd make me go straight home.

The trouble with looking for a kitten is that you really can't be sure she's not there, even when you've looked really hard. Kittens are mischievous creatures and love to play hide-and-seek. But after a good ten minutes of searching, I was pretty sure Halo wasn't in the churchyard. I went on to the park.

Mum and Dad don't like me to go the park on my own. It's quite big and people have been mugged there. But I was so worried about Halo that I didn't care. I ran across the play area, calling her name, and then hurried to the pond. I was dreading seeing a little body floating on the surface but couldn't even get close because the pond had overflowed and the ground around it had turned into a swamp. I stared at it in despair and then gave myself a mental shake. Halo

wouldn't have gone that way. She hates paddling.

Just then, I heard something I was dreading: my name being called. My mum must have followed me.

'Jenni! Jenni!'

I swung round. It didn't sound like my mum, but who else would have come to look for me? A small figure was splodging towards me.

'Jenni! Wait! Please!'

It was Daisy. What on earth was she doing here? Never mind, perhaps she could help me find Halo. I was fed up with my vow of silence anyway.

Daisy's face was all pink and blotchy. She had been crying. Well, no surprises there and I hadn't time to ask why – it was getting darker all the time.

'I've lost Halo,' I said. 'But I don't think she can be here – it's too wet.'

Daisy gulped. 'I'll help you look,' she said. 'Would she have gone down by the river?'

'I don't know,' I said. 'I don't know where she

goes when she's exploring.'

'Well, we could try down there,' said Daisy. 'If you're not scared.'

'Of course I'm not scared,' I said. 'Saints don't do scared. Let's go.'

There's a path that winds down to the river. It's a lovely place to picnic and there are shallow places where you can paddle. Willows grow all along the edges – it's so peaceful in the summer.

The river didn't look peaceful today. Nobody in their right mind would have wanted to paddle; you could easily be swept off your feet.

'I can hear something,' said Daisy.

So could I. A kitten. Mewing piteously.

'It's near the water,' said Daisy. 'Over there, where the willows are.'

It didn't take me long to find Halo. Rescuing her was another matter. She was a little way up a tree, clinging to a branch which hung out over the water. One of those loops of plastic that you get on six-packs had caught in the tree and she had put her head through it. She was well and truly stuck!

'Oh no!' I said. 'How am I going to get her out of there?'

'I'll hold you while you lean out,' said Daisy. 'Go on – be quick. It'll be too dark to see soon.'

'But I'm heavier than you,' I said. 'D'you think you can manage?'

'I'm stronger than you think,' she said, 'what with looking after my mum.'

I didn't stop to think what that meant but let her grab me round the waist. Then I inched forward as far as I could on the slippery bank. There was no chance of me getting Halo out of the plastic loop; I would have to unhook it and disentangle her later. I stretched and stretched and stretched. If they put any saints on the rack, then I think I know what it felt like.

'It's no good,' I said. 'I can't reach.'

'If I hang onto you with just one arm, you'll be able to stretch a bit further,' said Daisy.

It sounded dodgy to me but I hadn't much choice. Feeling far less safe than before,

I stretched again. This time my fingers reached the plastic loop. Just a little bit further and it was in my hand. All I had to do now was unhook it and get back – but that was when disaster struck. It must have been the jerk as I unhooked it – or my foot losing its grip on the bank. Whatever it was, I slipped and Daisy couldn't hold me. The next moment, I was in the water and so was Halo. And it was *so* scary.

I forced my face up out of the dark, rushing water and groped about for the bank – but I couldn't let go of Halo, and with only one hand I couldn't get a grip. I was floundering in water that wasn't very deep, but was pulling me so strongly that the bank was getting further away. Praying suddenly didn't seem boring at all. It was just the obvious thing to do. I thought of St Christopher battling to carry people across the river. I would never be any good at that but surely God could at least help me get out? If only I had a big stick to help me, like St Christopher did, to get a grip.

Well, I didn't have a big stick but I did have Daisy. She had flung an arm round a willow and was reaching out for me.

'Grab my hand, Jenni,' she was shouting, 'Quickly! I can pull you back!'

'You'll fall!' I spluttered.

'No I won't!'

I scrabbled and splashed about and managed to get a firm enough foothold to lunge towards Daisy. Our fingers met and mine closed, gripping hers for all I was worth. She pulled, I scrabbled, and moments later, I was safe on the bank. It took us a moment to remember Halo but she hadn't forgotten us. She was soaked, bedraggled and still caught in her plastic noose but she was furiously angry, clawing and scratching at my wrist.

Daisy took her off me and snuggled her into the front of her coat.

'Thank you, Daisy,' I gulped. 'I think you saved our lives. And after I've been so mean to you too.'

'It was just lucky I was here,' she said. 'Come

on, we'd better go. Both our mums are going to go mad.'

'Too right,' I said. I suddenly felt very feeble and not like a brave, bold saint at all. Super hero? Forget it. Facing my mum was going to be quite scary enough for me.

It wasn't until the next morning, when I woke up, that I remembered that Daisy had been crying when I met her. And I'd never asked her what she was doing in the park. I knew her mum was just as bothered as mine about her going there on her own.

'Daisy,' I said, when I found her in the playground at school. 'Why were you crying last night? And why were you in the park?'

Daisy looked away. 'Doesn't matter,' she said.

'No, tell me. I won't tell anyone else, I promise.'

She looked at me. 'Really promise?' she said.

'Really promise' I said.

'My mum's ill,' said Daisy. 'All the time. She has something called MS.* Sometimes she's not

**MS, or multiple sclerosis, is a disease that affects the body's nervous system. Some people with MS can feel well for some of the time but others feel poorly all the time.*

so bad, sometimes she can hardly get out of bed. Sometimes I just get really fed up with it. That's when I go to the park – just to get away. I know I shouldn't but I do.'

Suddenly it all made sense. All that Daisy had said, what other people had said, why there wasn't much money.

'Why don't you tell people?' I asked.

Daisy shrugged. 'Because they say things.'

I thought of Jade and Shelley. Yes, they were quite capable of teasing Daisy, even about something as terrible as that.

'I wouldn't say things,' I said stoutly.

'Well, you can't, can you?' she said. 'Not if you're going to be a saint!'

I looked at Daisy. She might look like a feeble little wimp but I reckoned when it came to saintliness, she beat me hands down. She was strong and brave and daring and I'd never heard her say an unkind thing to anyone. I thought about how I'd treated her recently and I reckoned that for a saint-in-training, I had a long way to go.

'Come on,' I said, grabbing her hand. 'Let's go and play "saints" till the whistle blows. Which saint shall we do?'

'Rose of Lima,' said Daisy. 'She sounded really good fun.'

I gulped and took a deep breath. 'Daisy,' I said, grabbing her other hand as well, 'there's something I should have told you before about Rose of Lima…'

Daisy grinned. 'I know,' she said. 'I looked her up. You can be Rose, I'll be the brother that builds her a hut to live in. But first I'm going to collect some nettles. Did you know she stuffed her gloves with them? I brought a pair specially for you!'

'Daisy, I…'

Daisy burst out laughing. 'Your face!' she said. 'I was joking, you idiot! Come on, we never did St Paul either. I'll be him and you can be the horse that he's riding. You're bigger than me.'

Huh! Maybe Daisy isn't quite so saintly after all! I think we've both got a long way to go!

Jenni's Guide to the Saints

Part 2

St Margaret

A princess who escaped to Scotland and married King Malcolm when William the Conqueror took over England. King Malcolm was rough and war-like but Margaret soon changed things. He learnt not to notice how much of his money she spent feeding the hungry!

St Laurence

St Laurence worked for the pope and cared about poor people. When he refused to obey the Romans, they 'grilled' him over a fire. He's the patron saint of cooks!

St Patrick

When he was 16, Patrick was captured by pirates and sold as a slave to an Irish Chieftain! Scary! When he finally escaped back to England, he trained as a priest – and promptly returned to Ireland to tell people about Jesus!

St Paul

Paul did **terrible** things to Christians until he had a vision of Jesus on the road to Damascus. Then terrible things happened to **him** – he was shipwrecked, put in prison, beaten and executed! He travelled miles, telling people about Jesus - in fact, it's mostly down to Paul that we know about Jesus today.

St Joan of Arc

Joan, a young teenager, heard voices from God telling her to help the French prince to fight the English. The English didn't like being beaten, especially by a girl, so they said she'd listened to the devil's voice and burned her alive.

St Christopher

No one really knows if Christopher existed. There's a great story about him carrying Jesus across a river without knowing who he was. Christopher did something good without realizing it, because he tried so hard to do the right thing. I keep hoping that might happen to me!

St Peter

One of Jesus' special friends and always the first to open his big mouth – a bit like me, really. He made some terrible mistakes but he spent his life telling people about God until he was captured and crucified for his beliefs – upside down!

Rose of Lima

The first American saint, she believed that by suffering she could make up for the sins of other people – so she lived in a shack in the garden, wore hairbands made of thorns and gloves full of nettles! She also helped the poor, the native Indians and the slaves – which makes more sense to me!

St Stephen

The first man to die because he believed in Jesus. He told the Jewish leaders exactly what he thought of them for killing Jesus – and they stoned him to death! Worse, St Paul (then called Saul) watched! With his last words, Stephen asked God to forgive his killers. How amazing is that?

St Sebastian

This one's really nasty! Sebastian objected to the Roman emperor killing Christians. Mistake! The emperor made his archers use him for target practice! Sebastian survived and promptly objected again! This time he was clubbed to death.

St Catherine of Alexandria

No one knows if Catherine really existed but there are great stories about her. I like the one where the Roman emperor (who was already married) wanted her to be his wife. He got some wise men to persuade her that her Christian beliefs were rubbish but she convinced them that they were wrong instead!

St Apollonia

A brave old lady who lived in Alexandria where a bloodthirsty mob was killing all the Christians. When she was caught, they pulled out all her teeth and threatened to throw her on a bonfire unless she gave up her belief in Jesus. So she jumped into the flames herself! No one was going to boss her about except God!

St Clare of Assisi

Clare thought Christians should live simple lives – so she ran away from home to join St Francis. She cut her hair short, wore sandals and a rough robe. She set up a group of nuns who never ate meat or wore shoes and didn't own anything – not even a toothbrush! There are still nuns today called the Poor Clares – but I think they have toothbrushes.

St Thérèse de Lisieux

Thérèse became a nun when she was 15! She died when she was only 19 but is famous for writing a book called **The Little Way** which explains how anyone can serve God in little ways without complaining. I'll have to work on it!

For St George, St Cuthbert and St Sergius, see *Saint Jenni: Animal Crazy*.